SeDUCTiVe ESPIONaGE

THE WORLD OF YUKI 7

created by **KEVIN DART** written by **ADA COLE**

Published in the United States of America, July 2009
First edition

Published by Fleet Street Scandal
For information contact info@fleetstreetscandal.com

www.fleetstreetscandal.com

ISBN: 0-9823391-0-0
ISBN 13: 978-0-9823391-0-7

Printed in China through Global PSD

dedicated with love to ELIZABETH MAY DART (1933-2008)

CONTENTS

the world of YUKI 7

Introduction by Michiko Ito

Like many of you who hold this book in your hands, I grew up with Yuki 7. In 1964, I was seven years old, and my grandfather, Shigeru Ito, took me to see my very first film. I was too young to understand at the time that the film belonged to him, that he worked closely with my 'Uncle' Hitori and his friend Kenji-san to make it. I was, like many people on that hot July afternoon, simply slipping into a cool and dark theatre with my grandfather to enjoy an afternoon movie.

Up until that point, I don't think I ever sat still so long or behaved so well in my life. I was transfixed by Yuki 7, fascinated by her space-age gadgetry, enchanted by her beauty, triumphant when she vanquished the bad guys - or girls in this case. After the film, my grandfather and I went to have ice cream. He asked me question after question about what I had seen. I talked non-stop. I remember the afternoon so clearly, because I had his absolute attention. He spoke to me as though I was an adult, and

CONTINUED ▶

YUKI 7 OUTWITS HER PURSUERS ON
THE ROAD TO DIAMOND EYE'S LAIR
"A KISS FROM TOKYO" FILM STILL, 1964
Courtesy of Stephane Coedel,
Cinematographer

my opinion mattered. I didn't realize for years how much was at stake when the first Yuki 7 film came out, and how much my young opinion *did* matter.

So much of filmmaking takes place in a vacuum. Before the release, a small fortune was poured into Yuki 7 on the basis of what can reasonably called a hunch. All those involved were steadfastly confident in what they were creating - they believed in every joke, every dramatic climax, every explosion and each line of dialog. But all of this hung on a singular uncertainty - was the world ready for a female spy as a lead character?

My conversation with my grandfather has faded to whispers in my memory, but I remember his final question as he wiped ice cream off my chin, hands, and shirt. "So, my little dear, tell me this last thing. Do you want to see Yuki 7 again?" I said, "Oh, *Ojiisan*, yes! Can we? Right now?" The smile on his face was unforgettable.

During the era in which I was born, it was expected that my life's work would be husband and family, as my mother's was before me, and her mother's before her. Yuki 7, however, was part of a cultural revolution, especially for women. I learned, along with an entire generation of girls wearing those signature white earrings, that my future was mine to create.

Eventually, I persuaded my grandfather to allow me to work

▲ KIMIKO SUZUKI AUTOGRAPHED HEADSHOT, 1965

I WORE A PAIR OF SMALL WHITE EARRINGS TO REMIND ME OF MY ORIGINAL INSPIRATION,

YUKI 7

◄ KENJI MIMOTO, ON LOCATION SHOOT, 1965
▼ KIMIKO SUZUKI ON SET, 1964

for International Productions. It wasn't easy to be a woman in a man's world. But I was committed to becoming a producer, just like my grandfather. On the days when the pressure seemed the most unbearable, and my dream seemed impossible, I wore a pair of small white earrings to remind me of my original inspiration, Yuki 7.

In the last 30 years I've been involved in many films, but my fondest movie memory remains that first afternoon with my grandfather and *A Kiss from Tokyo*, when Yuki 7 showed me my first glimpse of a limitless future.

Before the films became a sensation with a cult following that spanned the globe, it was just us, the early fans, who loved Yuki 7 and returned to the theatre to see her time and time again. *Seductive Espionage: The World of Yuki 7* is a wonderful collection of stories and memorabilia celebrating an epic film series, but for fans like you and me, it's like a family album, full of happy memories. I hope that you enjoy it as much as I do.

Michiko Ito, President of International Productions

February 9, 2009

Tokyo, Japan

a KISS FROM TOKYO

1964

Yuki 7 dashes around the world in hot pursuit of the tantalizingly tricky Diamond Eye, who is stealing parts and plans and leaving behind a path of murdered scientists in her quest to build a missile inside her volcanic lair. Yuki finds former classmate and good girl Sandy 6 working for the vampy villainess and chases her off, but not before Diamond Eye has the final part in her hot little hands. Yuki 7 has to infiltrate the rumbling volcano and stop the launch with only minutes to spare.

the birth of a heroine

Excerpt from "The Mimoto Story"

YUKI 7 RECIEVES AN ASSIGNMENT ON THE VIDEO PHONE IN HER SECRET HEADQUARTERS

For longtime fans, the story of Yuki 7 is an epic tale, spanning decades and dozens of films, spinoffs, comics, and novels. The international success of Yuki 7 is undeniable in retrospect, but what many fans do not realize is that her beginning was serendipitous, and if it weren't for the passion and vision of a few key people, she might never have existed at all.

In the early 1950's, longtime friends and business partners Hitori Kojima and Shigeru Ito formed a small scale

CONTINUED ▶

SHIGERU AND HITORI ITO KOJIMA PRESENT KENJI MIMOTO'S

A KISS FROM TOKYO

WITH
MEGUMI GOU
AND LUCY DE SOTO

STARRING
KIMIKO SUZUKI
AS
SECRET AGENT
YUKI 7

presented in
CINESCOPE®
THE ASTOUNDING
VIEWING EXPERIENCE

COLOR BY
CHROMALUX®

INTERNATIONAL PRODUCTIONS

film studio called International Productions. Japanese film was just beginning to enjoy worldwide acclaim, with Kurosawa's *Rashomon* earning an Academy Award in 1950. Ito and Kojima hoped to profit by creating additional films on popular themes. They were immediately successful, as the public began to embrace moviegoing as a family pastime and the awards bestowed on Japanese films as a point of national pride.

In the early 60's, Japanese audiences were becoming more interested in films from the U.S. and International Productions set their sights on creating Japanese versions of popular Hollywood films. Almost immediately, Kojima discovered the James Bond series. Although completely new and arguably off to a rough start, the series impressed Kojima with its potential. Ito initially disliked the first Bond film, *Dr. No*, but after repeated urging from Kojima, read and admired Ian Fleming's books and thought the idea of a handsome hero fell in neatly with the samurai tradition and would have widespread appeal.

Once committed to the idea, they were unable to interest any directors in the spy film theme. In 1963, Kojima reluctantly agreed to shelve the project and flew to the U.S. in search of other ideas. Just two weeks later, a young unknown named Kenji Mimoto applied at the studio. Mimoto had attended The Film School of Tokyo, but to date had only acted as an assistant director on a few obscure films and directed two episodes of the short-lived *Flash Girl Five* action TV show.

CONTINUED▶

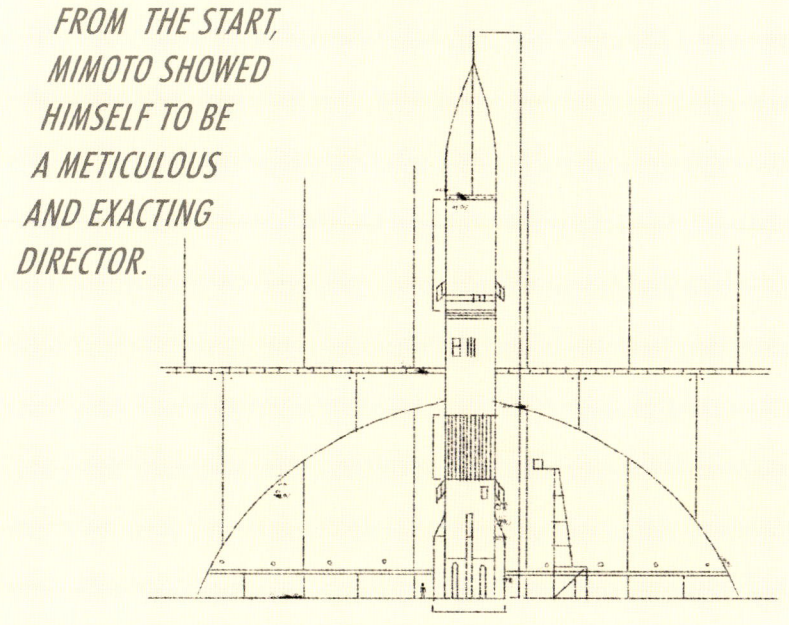

FROM THE START, MIMOTO SHOWED HIMSELF TO BE A METICULOUS AND EXACTING DIRECTOR.

▲ MISSILE PAD SET DESIGN, 1963
◀ "A KISS FROM TOKYO" ENGLISH RELEASE POSTER, 1964
▼ K79 PISTOL BY BILL MATSUDA AND YUKI DRESS BY DAN TANAKA, 1964

On his trip, Kojima saw *From Russia with Love*, and his passion for the project was rekindled, and some say, bordered on the obsessive. When he returned to Japan, he called Mimoto in for an interview and hired him after a mere 20 minutes of conversation. Ito saw the entire project as a gamble, so he later persuaded Kojima to agree to initially limit the project to a 15 minute preview with a shoestring budget.

From the start, Mimoto showed himself to be a meticulous and exacting director. He screen tested all the male leads under contract with International and rejected them all outright. Casting calls ended in frustration, and options slimmed to nothing.

With only 2 weeks left to salvage the project, Mimoto bumped into an unknown actress named Kimiko Suzuki at the post office. Struck by her beauty and spark, he persuaded her to screen test the following week. "It was magic on film," Mimoto would later recall,

◄ "A KISS FROM TOKYO" FRENCH RELEASE POSTER, 1964
▼ SET DESIGN FOR THE MINISTER OF SCIENCE OFFICE, 1963

...IT WAS RISKING ALL OF THE FUTURE OF YUKI 7.

produit par
SHIGERU ITO
et HITORI KOJIMA

présentés dans CINESCOPE | couleur par CHROMALUX

BON BAISER DE TOKYO

réalisé par KENJI MIMOTO
avec
KIMIKO SUZUKI
dans le rôle de
YUKI 7 le Mystérieux Agent International

INTERNATIONAL PRODUCTIONS

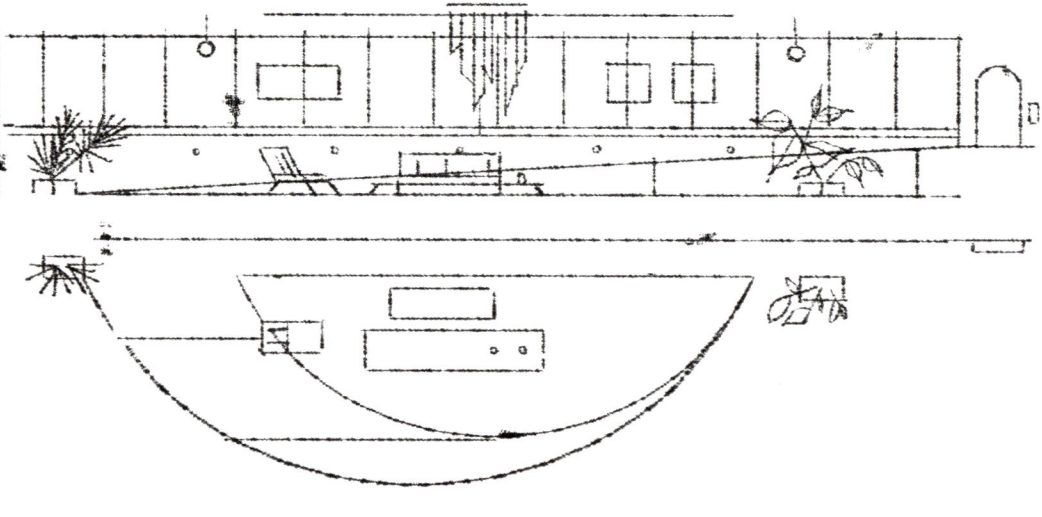

"all at once it came together in my mind. This film, and possibly many more, could be breathtaking and truly original with a female lead."

Ito and Kojima were enchanted by Suzuki, but extremely skeptical that audiences would embrace the idea of a female spy without a male counterpart. Having built their success by replicating existing formulas, they were hesitant to do anything original, especially with an unproven director at the helm. Mimoto persuaded them that International had the potential to move from industry follower to a much more lucrative position as leader. Kojima and Ito eventually relented and allowed Mimoto to produce

the preview with Suzuki.

Mimoto immediately ordered the construction of Yuki 7's elaborate headquarters, a swinging, modern office space of grand proportions and expensive designer appointments. He spent nearly double his budget on the construction of the set alone. Later, he would comment, "I needed Kojima and Ito to see this film as a world-class production. Kimiko-san captured my imagination, and I needed to show [Kojima and Ito] that she had the power to hold the entire film in the palm of her hand. The set had to be constructed to fit my vision, and to do this the budget had to be ignored. I begin all of my films

CONTINUED ▶

"A KISS FROM TOKYO" JAPANESE RELEASE POSTER, 1964 ▶
A SCIENCE LAB EXPLODES AFTER A VISIT FROM SANDY 6
"A KISS FROM TOKYO" FILM STILL, 1964. Courtesy of Stephane Coedel, Cinematographer ▼

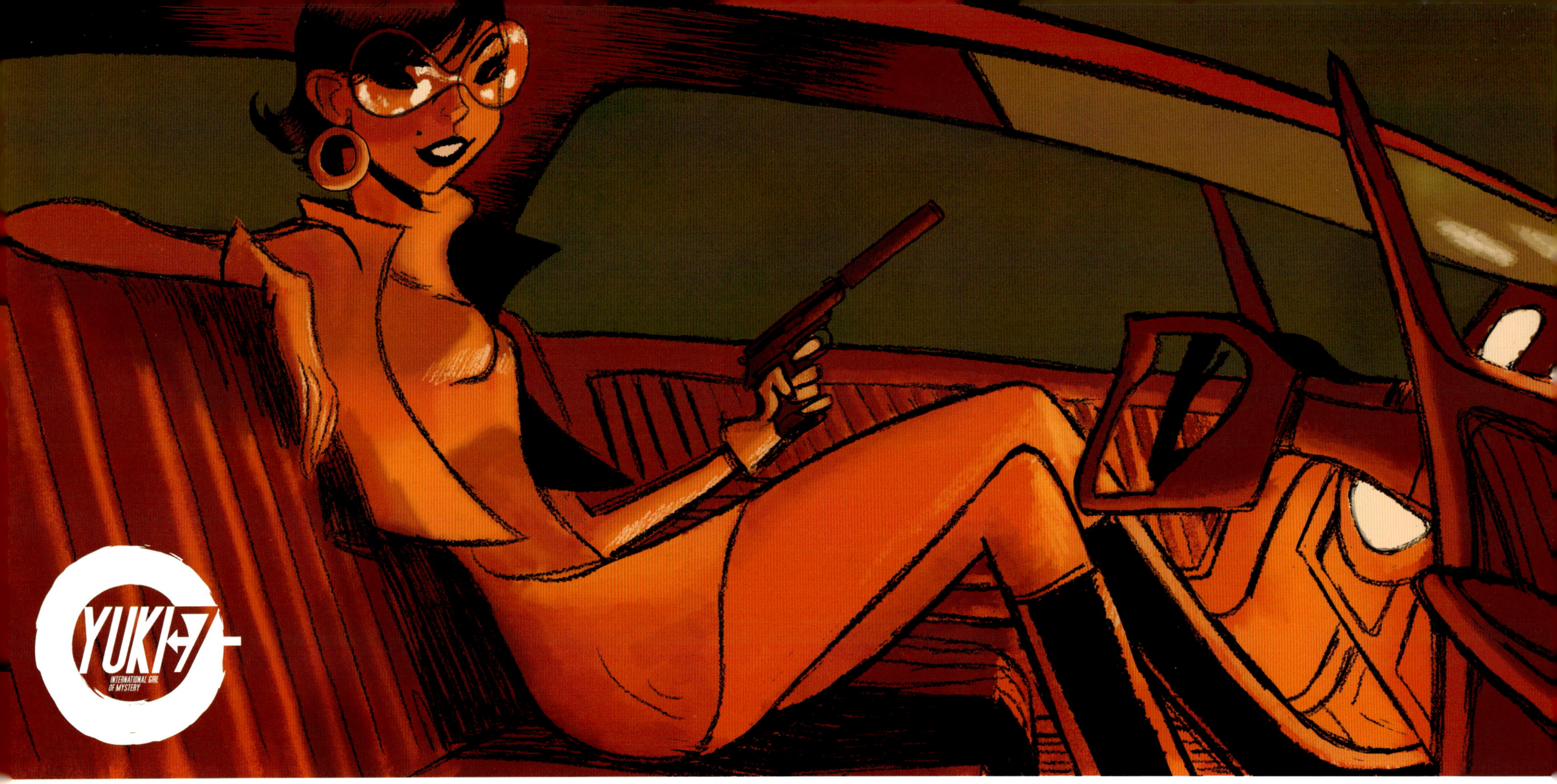

The ultimate in performance - in a beautiful package.

Yuki 7, the world's favorite spy, is as famous for bringing down bad guys as she is for her stunning good looks. Now she has a car that fits her style - and you can too. With a Vacu-matic transmission and a 370 horsepower Heron V-8 under the hood, the DeLine X8500 offers luxury without sacrificing the performance you need to pursue your target.

The X8500 - Yuki 7's official ravishing ride.

at the beginning – the first scene sets the tone, mood, and direction of the entire film. I wanted to open on headquarters that reflect the qualities of a great heroine the world would embrace, and to show Kimiko-san in charge and at ease in a grand setting. It was a great risk; it was risking all of the future of Yuki 7. But if we were to make this film, I wished to do so with confidence, from a place of victory."

Mimoto's risk paid off. Shocked and upset by the expenditure, Shigeru Ito rushed to the set and demanded to speak with Mimoto. To respond, Mimoto simply showed him approximately 4 minutes of film, depicting Yuki 7 accepting a commission from the UN to investigate the murders of several key scientists around the world. Ito silently departed the set, reel in hand.

Stories differ from this point forward, but it is commonly believed he sought out Kojima to watch the film again in private. What is known, however, is that within an hour, Mimoto received a phone call on the set and announced quietly to the staff that the film was greenlighted for full production. Mimoto was given free reign from that point forward.

Skirting direct questions about what exactly he did when he departed the set, Ito would later comment, "I like to believe I have built a career on spotting winners. Mimoto found a diamond, and like a jeweler he displayed her to her best advantage. I believed in Yuki 7, and am proud to have seen my belief bear fruit."

PORTRAIT OF KIMIKO SUZUKI AS YUKI 7, 1964
Courtesy of Daniel Arriaga, Photographer ▲

LUCY DE SOTO AS SANDY 6
"A KISS FROM TOKYO" FILM STILL, 1964
Courtesy of Stephane Coedel, Cinematographer ▶

DELINE AD, 1965
Courtesy of Ted Mathot, Art Director ◀

ELAN

THE MODERN WOMAN'S MAGAZINE · AUGUST, 1965

The Clothes We Want

By Edna Rowan

It has been a long, hot summer and ladies all over the country are ducking into supermarkets and movie theatres to beat the heat. So there's no way to miss the surprise smash hit from Japan, *A Kiss from Tokyo*, starring super spy-girl Yuki 7.

Yuki 7 gets a desperate call from the World Aeronautics Alliance: A path of missing missile parts and murdered scientists is spreading across the globe – can Yuki 7 save the day? Watch Yuki go up against the infamous villainess Diamond Eye, as things heat up inside a secret volcano lair.

Young girls love this fearless new role model from a foreign land, but grown women everywhere secretly covet her clothes. The practiced eye of a fashion maven can't help but notice the fantastic lines of Yuki's outfits. You don't have to be an international spy to know go-anywhere silhouettes in breezy fabrics are must-haves for the modern wardrobe.

We've heard hints that another Yuki 7 film is coming to the U.S. soon, featuring almost nothing but beautiful bikinis. To get to the bottom of these irresistible clothes, Elan called up Dan Tanaka, lead costume designer for Yuki 7.

E: Thank you so much for talking with us, Mr. Tanaka – we'll get right to the point. We love Yuki's look, and we want it for ourselves. When and where can we get it?

DT: Thank you. We are exploring ways to make Yuki's fashions available to the public. We recently spoke with fine swimwear company Sakura, and hope to release some of the outfits from *Danger is a Female*, the second Yuki 7 film.

E: And what about the gorgeous ring-necked number from *A Kiss from Tokyo*?

DT: Once we find a partner who can produce garments of Yuki 7 quality, we hope favorite outfits from the films will be widely available.

E: We can't wait. While we have you on the line, why don't you share with us your previous experience with women's fashion.

DT: Honestly, I have none.

E: None?

DT: Correct. I was hired by International to create clothing for a male lead. My designs were complete and fabric ordered when [Director Kenji] Mimoto unexpectedly changed the lead to a female. I had only a week to design and construct her signature outfit.

E: Astonishing! Tell us more.

DT: Well, there is not much more to tell. I sat in my study over a long weekend with the men's fabrics, plus a few scraps I was able to scrounge from local shops. The yoke is made from men's suiting, and the stripe is tie silk.

E: You turned scraps into finery that goes effortlessly from cat fight to catwalk - how is this possible?

DT: Well, I focused at first on architecture, which is the foundation of men's clothing. I created a structured dress that would convey strength and be well fitted from any angle. From there, I added softness and flow, to give the outfit feminine charm and highlight Yuki's beauty.

E: Everything men have, plus the undeniable allure of the feminine touch. Perfect for a lady making her way in a man's world! Elan ladies cannot wait to see your work pop up in shops here in the U.S., Mr. Tanaka.

Elan thanks Dan Tanaka for his time, and for bringing the world a fresh take on women's fashion. Don't miss A Kiss from Tokyo starring Kimiko Suzuki in theaters now, and look for Danger is a Female this September. Keep your eyes on the pages of Elan for the first news of Sakura swimsuits reaching our shores!

YUKI CHECKS HER WORLD MAP BEFORE DEPARTING ON A MISSION
"A KISS FROM TOKYO" FILM STILL, 1964
Courtesy of Stephane Coedel, Cinematographer

DANGER is a FEMALE

1965

The U.N. is desperate to find a plane full of diplomats that disappeared over the open sea. Yuki 7 rushes to the rescue and straight into an ambush! Bad girl Sandy 6 leads a clan of deadly scuba girls and a posse of pod-bots in a treacherous game of cat and mouse. Yuki hijacks a pod and escapes to a hidden cliff-side fortress. There, she finds a murderous heiress packing the diplomats into a plane to attempt escape. Yuki takes to the skies with the Sea Guard in tow and pulls off a daring midair rescue!

STARRING
KIMIKO
SUZUKI
AS
SECRET AGENT
YUKI-7

SHIGERU ITO AND HITORI KOJIMA PRESENT KENJI MIMOTO'S

DANGER is a FeMALE ®

WITH
KEIKO SHIBUYA
AND MIDORI HIROSHOBI

presented in
CINESCOPE ®
THE ASTOUNDING
VIEWING EXPERIENCE

COLOR BY
CHROMALUX ®

INTERNATIONAL PRODUCTIONS

the most expensive
7 seconds of film
ever made

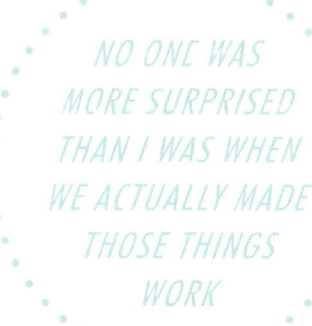

NO ONE WAS MORE SURPRISED THAN I WAS WHEN WE ACTUALLY MADE THOSE THINGS WORK

Courtesy of Bill Matsuda, production designer, as told to the author.

Mr. Mimoto would often bring in small objects he found and say, "Matsuda-san, come here, I have a pocket idea for you." For the original Yuki 7 headquarters, he brought me a tiny white porcelain bowl, so thin it was transparent. "This is the vision," he said, "the set should be like this bowl." So we built something curvy and white; opulent, but functional. Actually, the bowl is much like the ceiling lamps we made. Later, he brought a small cherry candy to me and said, "Make the chairs like this." So we did.

For *Danger is a Female*, however, he really challenged us. His very first 'pocket idea' was a ping pong ball. He skimmed it across the surface of the lobby fishtank, and told me that it should be a single man submarine, a little watercraft that looked futuristic and sinister. I immediately told him such a thing was impossible, and started detailing the technical issues we would encounter. He just smiled at me, and put the ball in my hand. "Think about it, Matsuda-san." he said. So I did, and no one was more surprised than I was when we actually made those things work.

Danger is a Female was one of the most technically challenging films of the decade. Approximately 70% of the scenes were filmed on or in water, requiring complicated rigging, boats, small aircraft, and a huge indoor pool. We lived at sea for weeks at a time, and it's a makeup miracle that the extras don't look as green on film as they were

CONTINUED▶

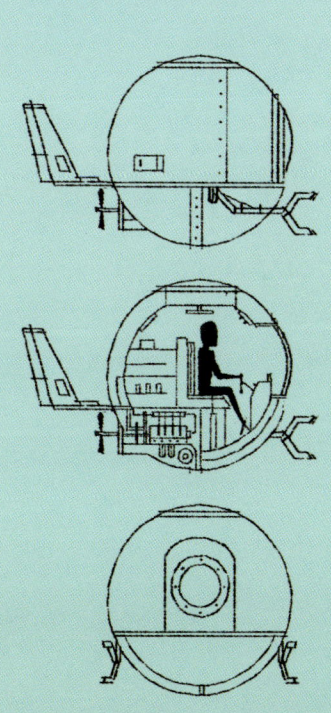

▲ POD-BOT DESIGN DETAIL, 1965
◄ CUSTOM MADE SCUBA GEAR, 1965
◄ OPPOSITE: "DANGER IS A FEMALE" ENGLISH RELEASE POSTER, 1965

伊藤茂 小島一人 提供
実元健次 監督
探偵由貴七号
危険な女
鈴木貴美子
偵探YUKI子
CINESCOPE® | CHROMALUX®

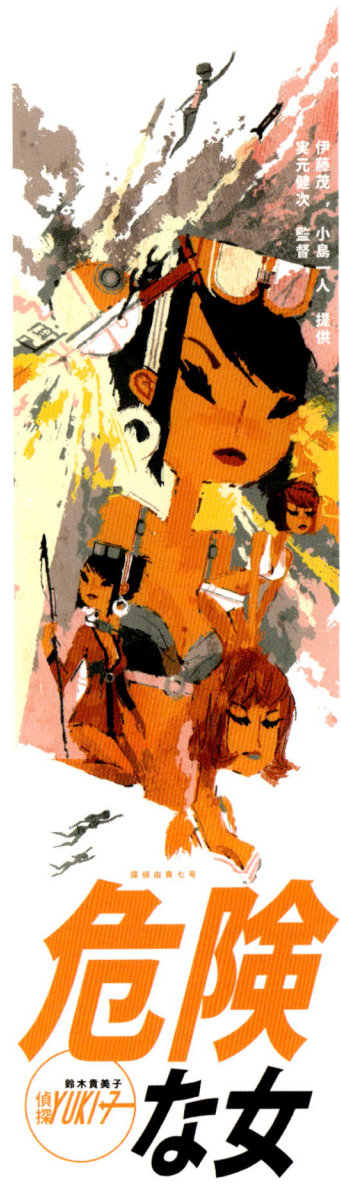

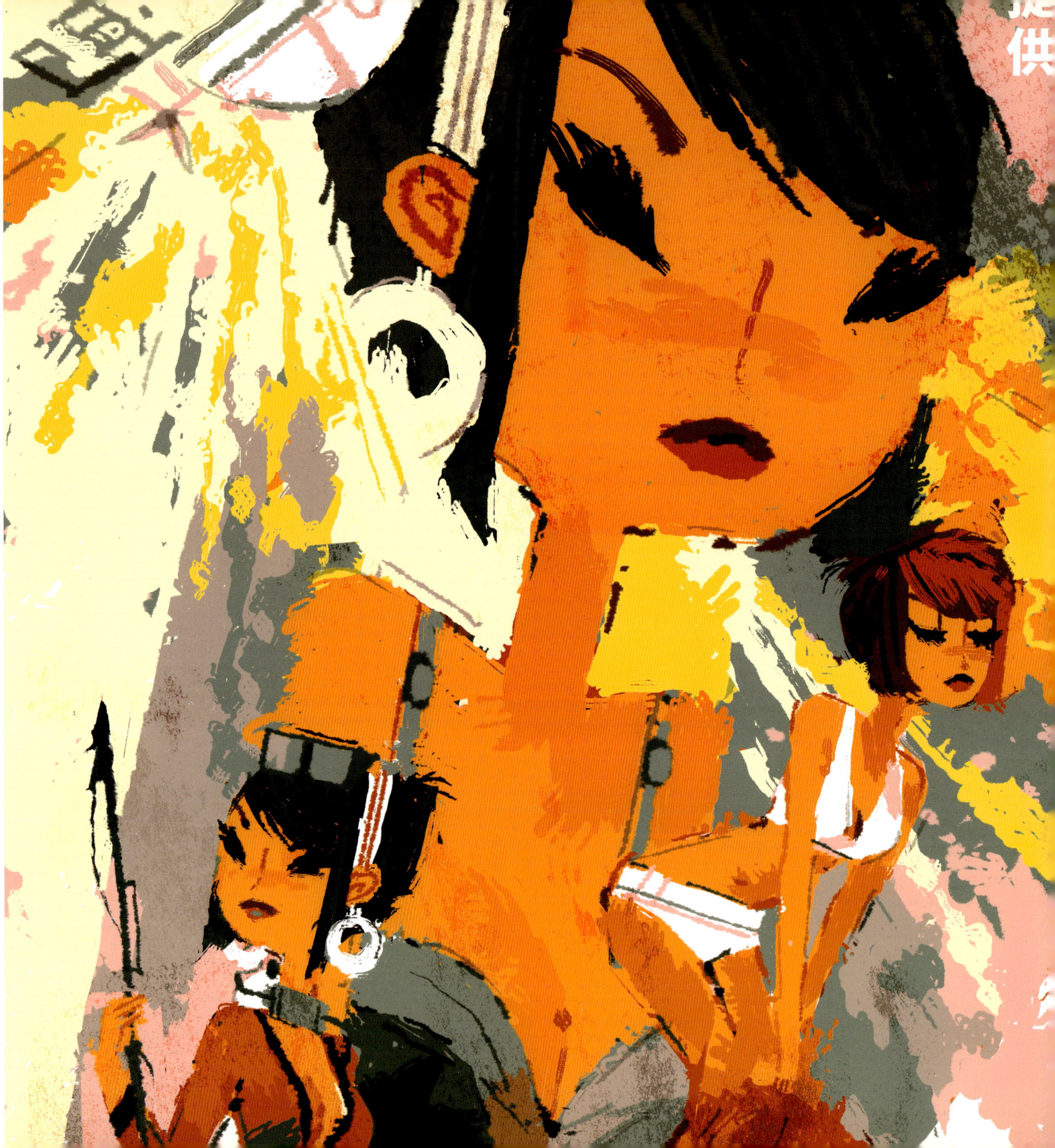

in real life. When designing sets from the middle of the ocean, it was challenging to be unable to simply build or buy whatever we wished. To create the lush underwater scenery, we spent a lot of time gathering seaweed and holding it like bouquets of balloons just off camera, or baiting schools of fish with little bits of rice.

What received the most attention in the media, though, was a scene from the end of the film. During the dramatic climax, Yuki 7 takes to the air in her custom white helicopter, supported by eight more helicopters from the Sea Guard. They chase down a luxury airliner carrying the kidnapped diplomats. We had five planes carrying cameras and crew capturing the action, for a total of 15 planes. The local air traffic controller was frantic. It took us an entire day of filming to capture the footage because of the constant need to refuel. Newspapers were quick to identify the scene as "the most expensive seven seconds of film ever made" - tallying the cost of the intensive training, aircraft, and fuel. Mr. Mimoto was very pleased - he has always urged every member of the crew to pull out all the stops for our loyal fans.

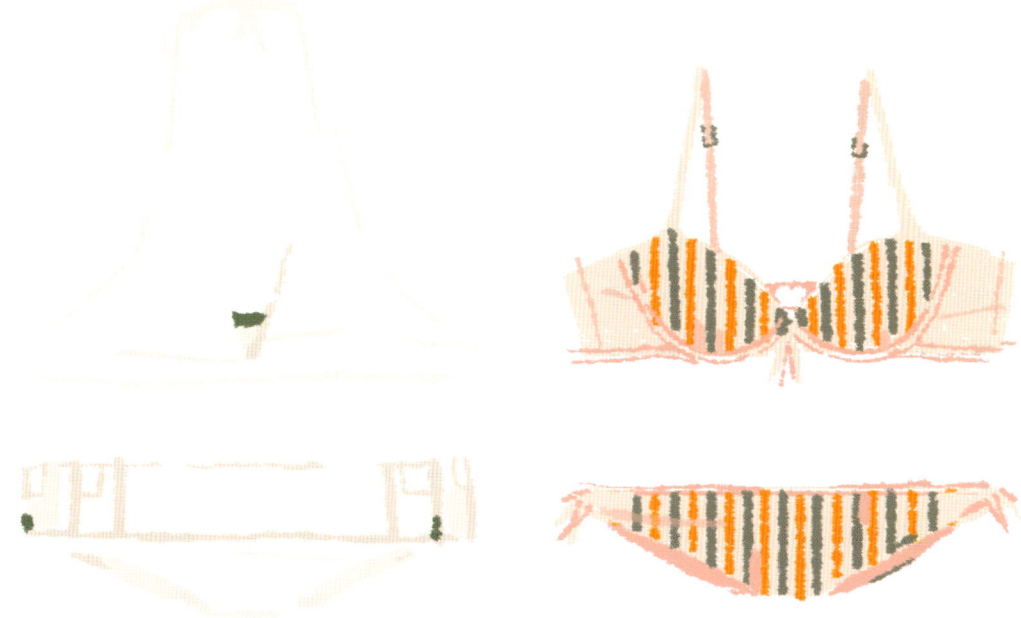

▲ BIKINIS BY DAN TANAKA IN ALLURON (LEFT) AND CHARMEUSE WITH HAND PAINTED STRIPES (RIGHT), 1965
◀ "DANGER IS A FEMALE" JAPANESE RELEASE POSTER WITH DETAIL, 1965
▶ "DANGER IS A FEMALE" FRENCH RELEASE POSTER, 1965

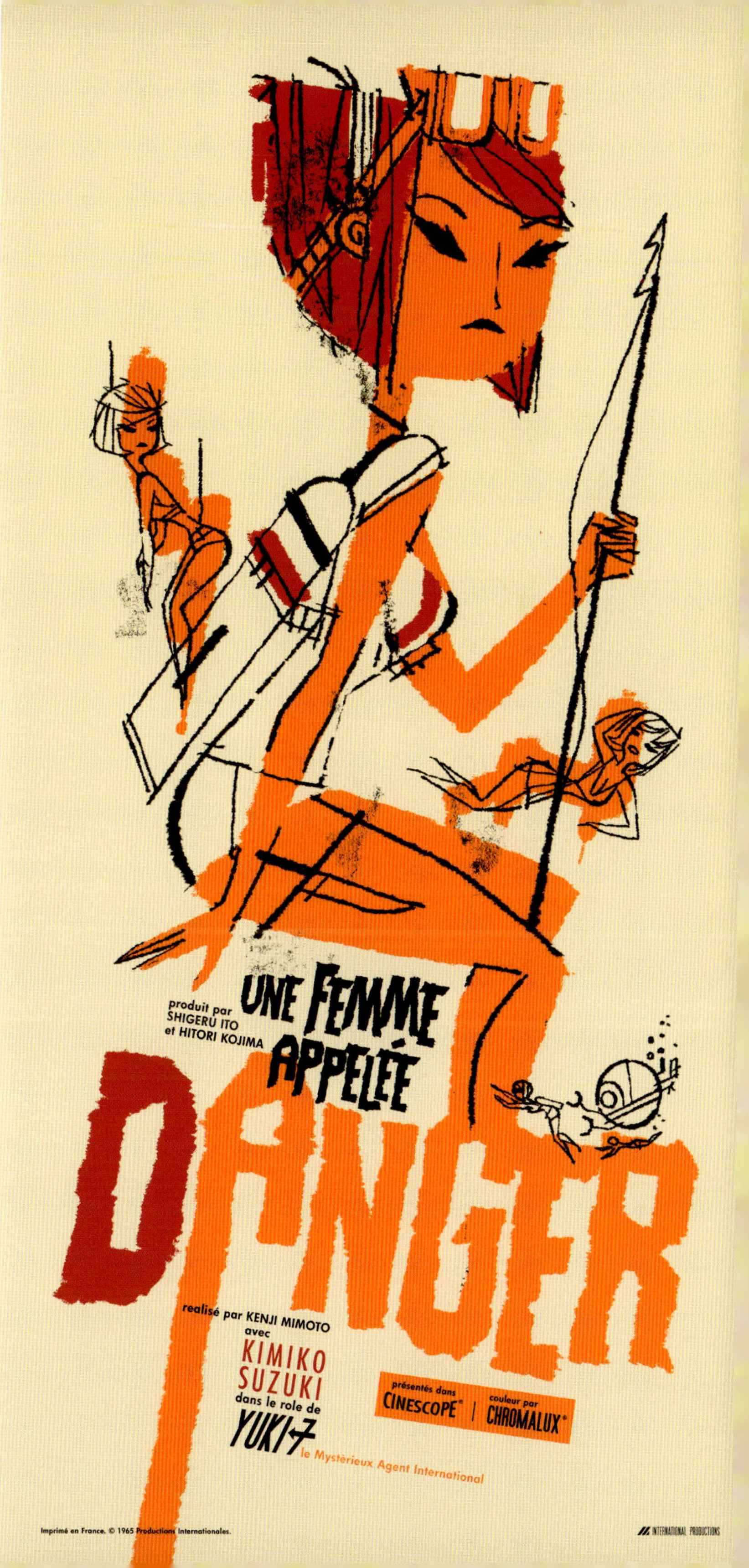

produit par SHIGERU ITO et HITORI KOJIMA
UNE FEMME APPELÉE
DANGER
réalisé par KENJI MIMOTO
avec
KIMIKO SUZUKI
dans le role de
YUKI 7
le Mystérieux Agent International
présentés dans CINESCOPE
couleur par CHROMALUX
Imprimé en France. © 1965 Productions Internationales.
INTERNATIONAL PRODUCTIONS

behind the BIKINI

All about the gorgeous swimsuits used in the summer hit "Danger is a Female"

Yuki 7's beautiful bikinis used throughout the film – 42 in all – were among the most valuable costumes ever made. Designer Dan Tanaka created the bikinis over the course of 8 months during pre-production, subjecting Suzuki to a grueling 120 hours of fitting. The suits were painstakingly handcrafted from the finest materials available including handmade lace, embroidered velvet, and silver and gold thread. They were kept in a small case – total weight a mere 27 lbs – and guarded personally by Tanaka until the release of the film. A famous photograph shows Tanaka at Heathrow with the case handcuffed to his wrist.

To prevent souvenir-seekers from snatching the tiny treasures, Suzuki was required to change completely and return the suit she was wearing to Tanaka. Tanaka would exchange it for the bikini needed for the next scene, so that any given time, only one bikini was outside of the case. In keeping with this tradition, museums hosting the Yuki 7 collection often display only one bikini at a time, usually next to the locked case.

Tanaka was distraught when a bikini was torn during a scene

TANAKA WAS
DISTRAUGHT WHEN
ONE BIKINI WAS
TORN...

where Yuki 7 scales the face of a cliff toward the murderous heiress. Finding the garment nearly irreparable and with the shooting schedule running tight, Mimoto made an uncharacteristic decision to change the storyboarding. Key scenes were re-shot from angles designed to camouflage the damage. Mimoto spent a significant amount of time editing this piece of film. In

his autobiography *Memories of My Films* he says, "The scaling of the cliffs was symbolic - Yuki 7 is struggling to climb the cliff, she is exhausted from her conflict with the deadly scuba girls, but still, she presses onward. I wanted to contrast her vulnerable but strong silhouette against the unforgiving and massive cliffs. For the first time I was forced to try to paint the picture in my

mind using only fragmented pieces. I think of it sometimes, and if I relived that time, I would have chosen simply to show the tear."

Dan Tanaka felt differently. Once filming was complete, he meticulously repaired the suit before returning it to the case.

ROMAN RENDEZVOUS

1966

A black market racketeer will stop at nothing to get their hands on a certain set of NASA blueprints, so Yuki 7 is called in to escort agent Lotus and the plans to Rome. In the waterways of Venice, The deadly Bikini Assassination Squad attacks, and the agents narrowly escape after a blistering swordfight. Back at the safehouse, Yuki discovers that the plans are fakes and Lotus is concealing the real plans in her lipstick – and is planning to slip them to the racketeer! Yuki and Lotus tangle but Yuki triumphs and delivers the real microfiche to grateful engineers in Rome.

bad girls

The Yuki 7 Villainesses

From exotic Diamond Eye to sworn enemy Sandy 6, the Yuki 7 films sparkle with a parade of beautiful bad girls. Collected quotes from the actresses who played Yuki's racy rivals reveal the complexity of these famous villainesses and details about life on the Yuki 7 set.

"Playing Diamond Eye was the first major role of my career, and where I learned the value of a director who has a clear picture of a character's life story and motivations. Diamond Eye is a brilliant scientist herself. In her mind, she is avenging her father by recovering inventions that were stolen from him. She's extremely willful, and when regular channels of justice failed, a drive for revenge came naturally. Mimoto would tell me very detailed stories about Diamond Eye's childhood, so that I could understand why she was the way she was. So when I read a pre-publication manuscript of [the book] *Diamond in the Rough*, much of the back story rang true. And as for Diamond Eye's divorce from science and descent into the criminal underworld of Monte Carlo - it's absolutely authentic to her character."

Megumi Gou plays Diamond Eye in A Kiss from Tokyo, *excerpted from an article in the April 1970 issue of Elan Magazine.*

CONTINUED ▶

DIAMOND EYE IN HER LAIR
"A KISS FROM TOKYO" FILM STILL, 1964
Courtesy of Stephane Coedel, Cinematographer

33

"The worst part about filming was the long hours. Mr. Mimoto was a perfectionist, and Kimiko Suzuki was absolutely tireless. I fell asleep between takes once. Remember the scene where I am in bed and Yuki is searching my things? She discovers the real microfiche in my lipstick and wakes me for a big confrontation. Well, Kimiko got her rummaging scene down in about five takes, which was just enough for me to fall all the way asleep in the prop bed. She ended up having to shake me to pieces to wake me up. At first, I thought Mr. Mimoto would be angry, but he ended up feeling the scene was more realistic with Yuki interrogating a groggy Lotus. After that though, I was very careful to keep drinking coffee after dinner!

The absolute best part about making a Yuki film of course was all of Dan Tanaka's gorgeous clothes! I kept every one of my costumes and I am just dying to be asked back again so I'll have more! "

Sophia Florentina, who plays Lotus in Roman Rendezvous, in an interview on the WKLD radio program "This Week At The Movies"

"According to the stories Mimoto told us, Sandy met Yuki when they were both about 8 years old at Elite Finishing School, an invitation-only school for gifted children. Sandy and Yuki are both orphans, and academic and playground rivals.

The school is actually a proving ground for recruitment into an elite fighting force called F.O.X.Y. Both Yuki and Sandy become agents after graduation, and are involved in sabotage, counter-espionage, and intelligence, which further hones their spy skills. Unlike Yuki, Sandy has no place to call home, so F.O.X.Y. becomes Sandy's surrogate family. Later, when Yuki discovers corruption and brings down the agency, Yuki is also destroying everything Sandy loves.

When the films begin, Sandy runs into Yuki while running errands for Diamond Eye, and from that point forward she actively seeks revenge. Sandy begins to move up in the underworld, eventually recruiting

CONTINUED ▶

AGENT LOTUS, 1966. Courtesy of Megan Brain, Costume Designer
EXCERPT FROM THE SYNDICATED YUKI 7 COMIC, 1967. Courtesy of Bill Presing, Comics Artist

YUKI 7
ART BY BILL PRESING
© KEVIN DART

SHIGERU ITO AND HITORI KOJIMA PRESENT KENJI MIMOTO'S

ROMAN RENDEZVOUS®

WITH MARI FUGAWA AND SOPHIA FLORENTINA

STARRING
KIMIKO SUZUKI
AS
SECRET AGENT
YUKI-7

presented in
CINESCOPE®
THE ASTOUNDING
VIEWING EXPERIENCE

COLOR BY
CHROMALUX®

▰ INTERNATIONAL PRODUCTIONS

her gang of Deadly Scuba Girls. She becomes bent on forcing Yuki into a dangerous situation that might lead to anything from disgrace to death, and from there she develops an elaborate kidnapping plot."

"The success of the films was wonderful, but for me, the greatest part was becoming friends with Kimiko Suzuki. Although we are absolutely venomous on screen, we were - and still are - best friends when the cameras aren't rolling. Kimiko is an incredibly lovely person. When we were filming *Temptress* in an old drafty castle, a tiny, ragged kitten showed up on set. Kimiko immediately started feeding him little tidbits and made a bed for him in the costume trailer. The next day, another two showed up, and on the third day, two more came. The kittens were all over the set and eating like kings. Kimiko set out a bowl of food for them, and soon discovered three more stray cats were dining when she had her back turned. It was maddening for Mimoto, but poor Kimiko didn't have the heart to turn them away. They kept coming and by the end of filming, we had eighteen cats and kittens to find homes for. It was the *Temptress* strays that started Kimiko's devotion to animal charities."

Lucy De Soto plays Yuki 7's longtime rival Sandy 6 in many of the Yuki films. From her book "Feeling Good Being Bad - My Life as Sandy 6"

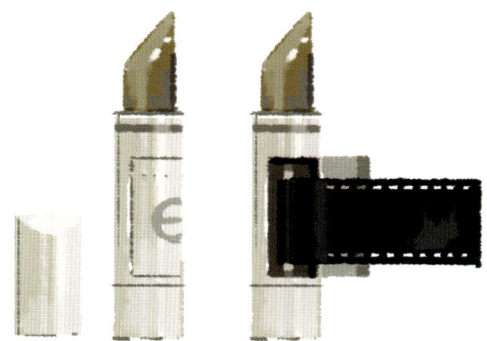

▲ MICROFICHE LIPSTICK PROP BY BILL MATSUDA, 1966
◄ "ROMAN RENDEZVOUS" ENGLISH RELEASE POSTER, 1966
► "ROMAN RENDEZVOUS" FRENCH RELEASE POSTER, 1966

Travel in *style!*

AIR PARIS

Making flights daily from London and Rome.

Whether rushing to an important press conference, or jetting off for a quiet vacation between movie shoots, international super star Kimiko Suzuki always chooses Air Paris, the world leader in comfort and reliability.

See Kimiko Suzuki in her new movie "Roman Rendezvous" this summer!

E L A N

THE MODERN WOMAN'S MAGAZINE · FEBRUARY 1966

sexy, savvy, SMART

why the world can't get enough of Yuki 7

> ON THE SURFACE, MIMOTO'S FILMS HAVE A LUSH AND INVITING CHARM.

◄ **COSTUME CONCEPT, 1965.**
Courtesy of Victoria Ying, Fashion Designer
◄ **OPPOSITE: AIR PARIS PROMOTION, 1966**

Globe-trotting IT girl Yuki 7 lights up the silver screen again this summer in *Roman Rendezvous*. Glam girls across the country loved Yuki 7 in *A Kiss From Tokyo* and *Danger is a Female*. What is it about her that lights our fire? We called up three elite members of the jet-set crowd and asked them, "Why does the world love Yuki 7?" – Here are their answers:

"I knew Yuki 7 was a hit when everyone in my family - young and old alike - gave *[A Kiss from] Tokyo* rave reviews. Yuki has a fire and a snap that's plain missing from the doe-eyed dolls in Hollywood these days. Men want ladies with bite, and women today want more to choose from in life than housewife, nurse, or teacher. A fab female international spy proves: girls today can throw the doors wide open on their futures. And why can't we look great and save the world at the same time? Yuki 7 is the poster girl for a new era."

Edith St. Claire, Hollywood reporter

"On the surface, Mimoto's films have a lush and inviting charm. We're drawn into the smooth, modern lines punctuated by jaw dropping explosions. But I think what keeps the films with us is their depth and subtle complexity. The average child gravitates to the action. But what remains in their hearts is the story of a tiny, orphaned girl from Hokkaido. Her enemy on the playground became her enemy on the battlefield. She struggles to protect the weak against the evil. The sparkling scenery and shattering action entertains us, but the epic story is what brings us – adult and child alike – back for more."

Eugene Markel, film critic

CONTINUED ►

"Yuki is the ultimate IT girl: sexy, savvy, and smart. She's gorgeous, of course, but it's her spine of steel that we admire… The costuming, for me, is an absolute A+. Yuki embodies my goal for women's fashion. You should be able to get dressed in five minutes, be comfortable for hours, and look like a million dollars every moment of your day. The outfits in the film are fearless without being scandalous - exactly where the modern woman wants to be "

Jean-Georges, fashion designer

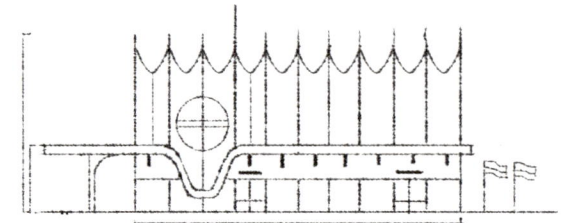 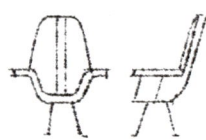

YUKI 7'S ROMAN SAFE HOUSE, 1966. *Courtesy of Chris Turnham, Set Designer* ▲
TOP: SET AND PROP CONCEPTS, 1966 ▲
OPPOSITE: FROM THE FIRST YUKI 7 NOVEL, 1967. *Courtesy of Jon Klassen, Illustrator* ▶

"Yuki watched from her motorcycle as the black car went
into the secret cliff cave."

to CaTCH a TEMPTRESS

1967

On a well deserved vacation to the coasts of Sardinia, Yuki 7 emerges from the ocean and smells chloroform on her towel - but realizes it a moment too late. When she awakens in a dark dungeon, a masked face appears and hypnotizes her. She's used like a puppet to steal valuable jewels. When the spell breaks, Yuki unmasks her captor - it's her longstanding foe, Sandy 6! After an epic battle that rages all over an ancient castle, Yuki emerges victorious and finds her place back on the beach.

STARRING
KIMIKO
SUZUKI
AS
SECRET AGENT
YUKI 7

SHIGERU AND HITORI
ITO KOJIMA PRESENT
KENJI MIMOTO'S

to CatCH a
TEMPTRESS

WITH
AKI ISHIKAWA
AND SAYAKA KOTANI

presented in
CINESCOPE®
THE ASTOUNDING
VIEWING EXPERIENCE

COLOR BY
CHROMALUX®

INTERNATIONAL PRODUCTIONS

spy fever!

owning a piece of Yuki 7

*(Excerpted and translated from doki*doki magazine, April 1966)*

Every month we get hundreds of letters on one subject: the delightfully enviable accessories inspired by our favorite star of the silver screen, Yuki 7. It all started when Midorikai released those darling earrings right after the release of *A Kiss from Tokyo*. Styled after the secret communicator earrings in the movies, they have a tiny radio and hidden speakers. They sold out in a snap and your letters came pouring in. Every girl in Japan wanted to know where to get them. We heard the most outrageous stories! Hundreds of girls went to fortune tellers to divine where the next shipment would arrive. Even the nightly news reported the latest sightings. Now we've all got a pair (or three!) and we are still loving the look.

It's common knowledge that Yuki 7 films come back from the theaters three to five seconds shorter in length - those single frames of film are hot collectibles. But our movie maven here at doki*doki has it on good authority that most copies of *Danger is a Female* come

CONTINUED▶

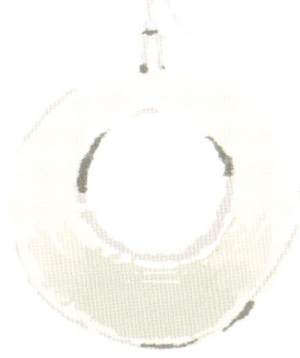 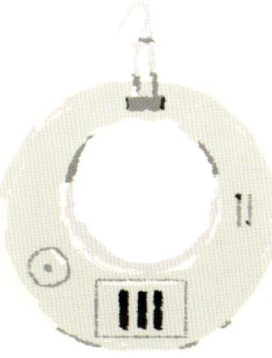

▲ YUKI 7 FEATHER DUSTER, 1966. Courtesy of Elizabeth Ito
◀ "TO CATCH A TEMPTRESS" ENGLISH RELEASE POSTER, 1967
▶ YUKI 7 COMMUNICATOR EARRINGS, 1964

探偵 由貴七号

INTERNATIONAL PRODUCTIONS 著作権 1964年 日本国印刷

back ten to fifteen seconds shorter! That's right girls, 240 to 360 frames out of each film are snipped and smuggled to eager fans! And you know those aren't shots of the airplanes that disappear - it's got to be the bikinis! Lucky for us, our favorite swimwear maker Sakura did a super job bringing us the sensational suits from the film.   We're over the moon for every single stitch in the collection and readers report a satisfying flutter of pulses whenever they are worn.

Fashionable home decorator Elizabeth Ito unveiled a flirty feather duster and an adorable concept for a sweet little Yuki 7 statuette in Paris this spring. We've had our ear to the ground about possible production dates, but have heard nothing about when they might hit stores. Our envy is palpable and our patience thin! Watch this space, ladies, because we're determined to be the first to report.

And you know that's true, readers, because have we got a surprise for you! We got a call from Midorikai this week - something very special is coming. In three months, every fortune teller and newscaster will have the same topic on their lips, but you heard it here first. The most heavenly accessory yet is on the way. Imagine yourself wearing Yuki 7's gorgeous garter… and groovier still, the holster will hold a tiny pink plastic gun that shoots little streams of cherry blossom perfume!

Yuki's garter is guaranteed to be a worldwide craze, and doki*doki readers have a chance to be first.   Midorikai has graciously agreed to send us a box before they ship to stores, and we're giving them away to 30 lucky girls. Borrow Papa's Polaroid and send us your best shot featuring you as Yuki 7. We'll publish our five favorites in a future issue, and draw another 25 lucky winners from all of the entries. Be sure to include your name and address on the back of your picture.

We'll see you opening night of *To Catch a Temptress*!

◄ "TO CATCH A TEMPTRESS" JAPANESE PROMOTIONAL POSTER, 1967

◄ OPPOSITE: "TO CATCH A TEMPTRESS" JAPANESE PROMOTIONAL POSTCARD, 1967

▼ YUKI 7 STATUETTE, 1966
Courtesy of Elizabeth Ito

E L A N

THE MODERN WOMAN'S MAGAZINE · APRIL, 1968

a visit from
kimiko
SUZUKI

(Excerpt from Elan Magazine)

E: Miss Suzuki, we are so happy to welcome you here to the United States and to see you on the red carpet at the Academy Awards last night.

KS: Thank you. It is my pleasure to visit again. It was a great honor to be a part of the ceremony.

E: You presented the award for Best Foreign Language Film; do you wish Yuki 7 had been in the running?

KS: Of course I am proud of my films, but there is so much beautiful work in the world and it was an honor to present the award to *Closely Watched Trains* [of Czechoslovakia]. Of course, we will always set our hearts on making the best film we can and it would be wonderful to be nominated.

E: Do you watch many American films? Were you rooting for anyone in particular last night?

KS. Oh yes, Mr. Mimoto insists that all the cast be familiar with films and stories from all over the world. Last night, I admit my heart was with *Cool Hand Luke*. Luke shows an unquenchable spirit. Although

CONTINUED ▶

YUKI 7 WAITS TO MEET HER INFORMANT IN TOKYO'S POSH 'CLUB GO-GO'
"A KISS FROM TOKYO" FILM STILL, 1964
Courtesy of Stephane Coedel, Cinematographer

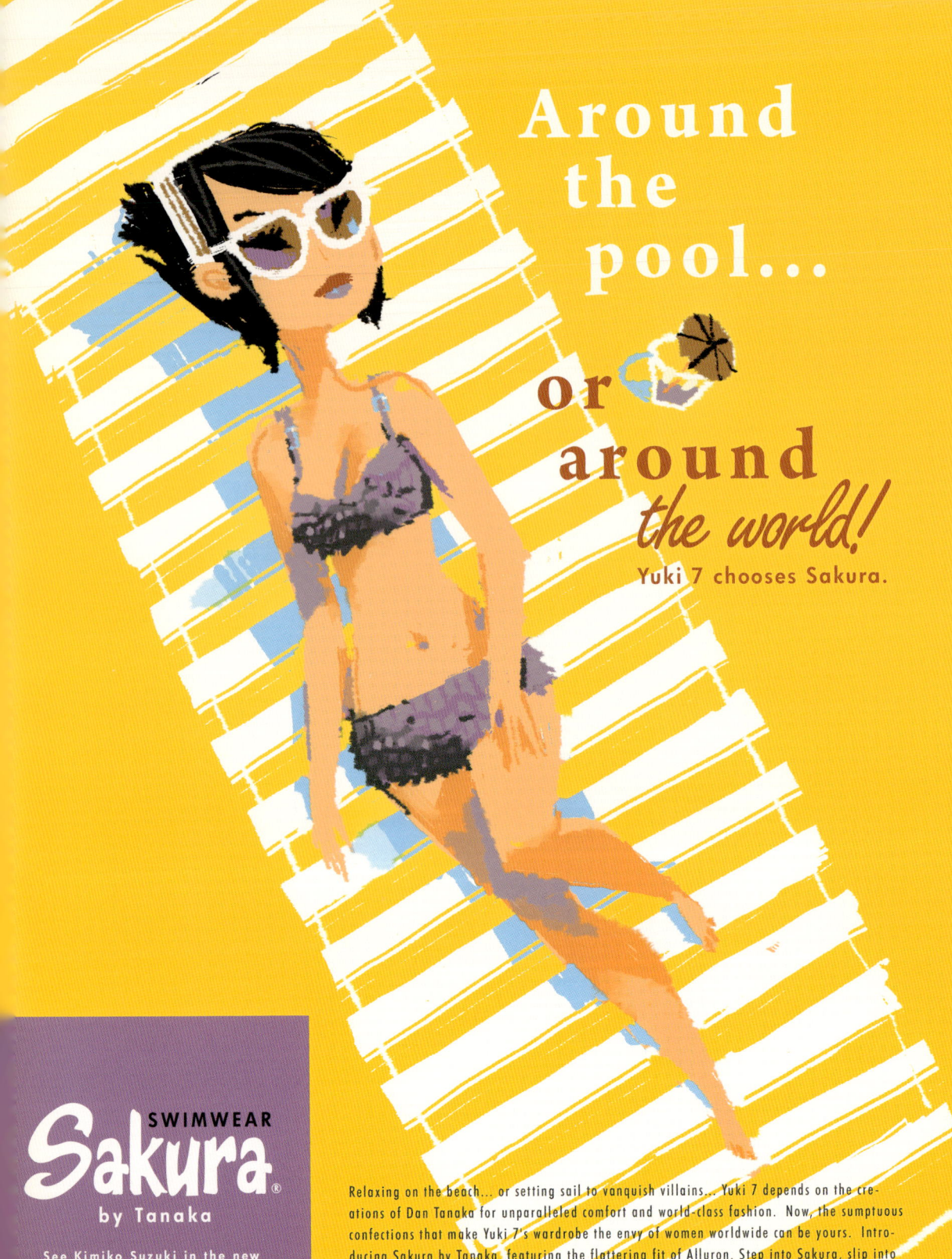

Around the pool...

or around the world!

Yuki 7 chooses Sakura.

his end is very lonely, he makes others happy when he can. I thought it was a very interesting kind of hero and a good story.

E: Did you meet any big stars?

KS: Oh yes! They were all very friendly and gracious. Even Mr. [Sean] Connery said hello to me.

E: Can we hope for a thrilling Spy vs. Spy movie in the future? Mr. Bond and Yuki 7?

KS: [Laughs] Who knows what the future will bring?

E: And finally, as the premier fashion magazine in the United States, we must inquire about your dress. You were certainly turning heads last night and no one has yet been able to name the designer. Will you satisfy our curiosity?

KS: Thank you. Of course, I can tell you: I made it myself. That is what modern times are about: defining your own style is the best way to be 'hip.'

Elan thanks Kimiko Suzuki of Yuki 7 fame for her time. Be sure to see the next Yuki 7 film coming to the U.S. in June. In To Catch A Temptress, Yuki 7 visits Sardinia on vacation and is kidnapped and brainwashed. Powerless, Yuki is forced to steal jewels from a heavily guarded palace. Can Yuki escape the grasp of the masked villainess behind it all? Find out this summer!

KIMIKO SUZUKI AT THE ACADEMY AWARDS, APRIL 10, 1968 ▶
SAKURA SWIMSUIT AD, 1968 ◀
FAR RIGHT: "TO CATCH A TEMPTRESS" FRENCH RELEASE POSTER, 1967 ▶

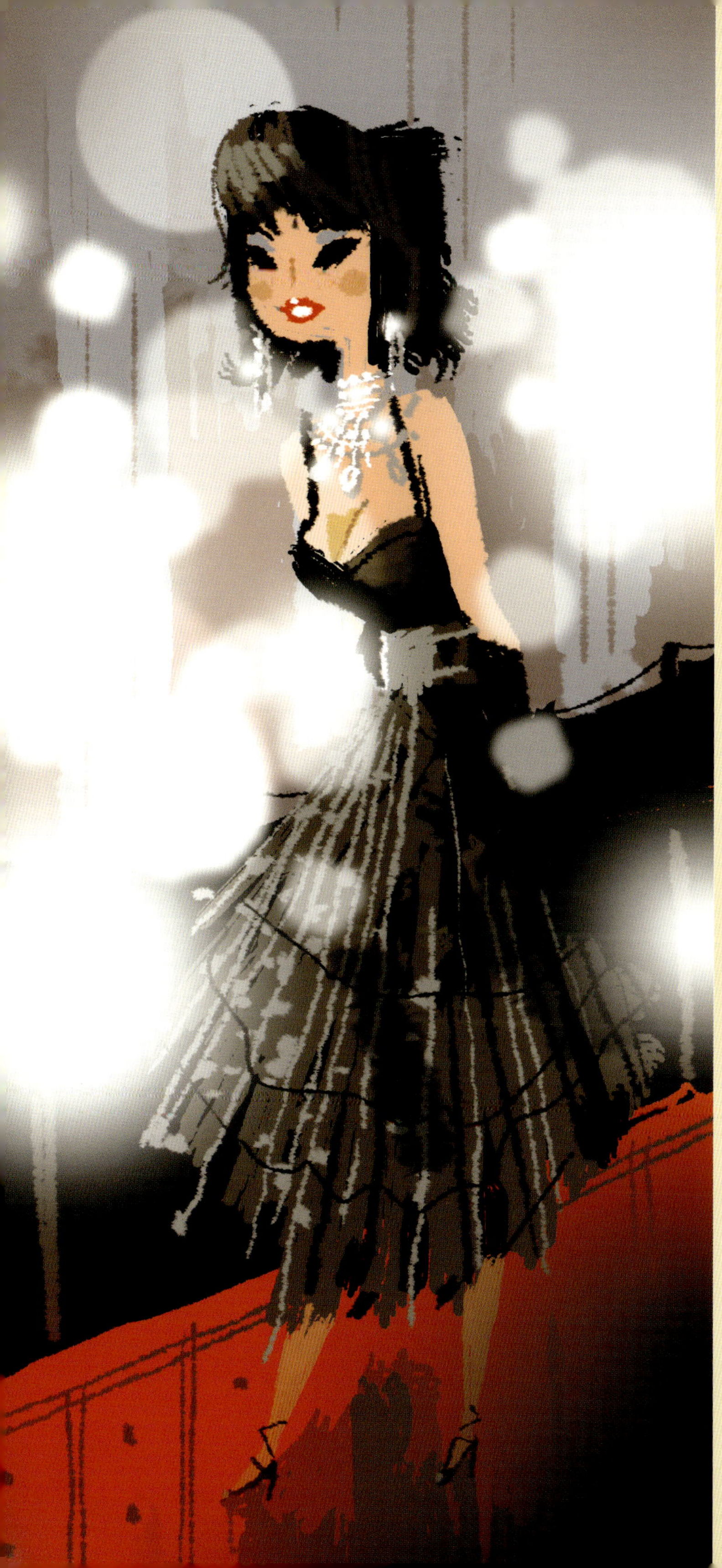

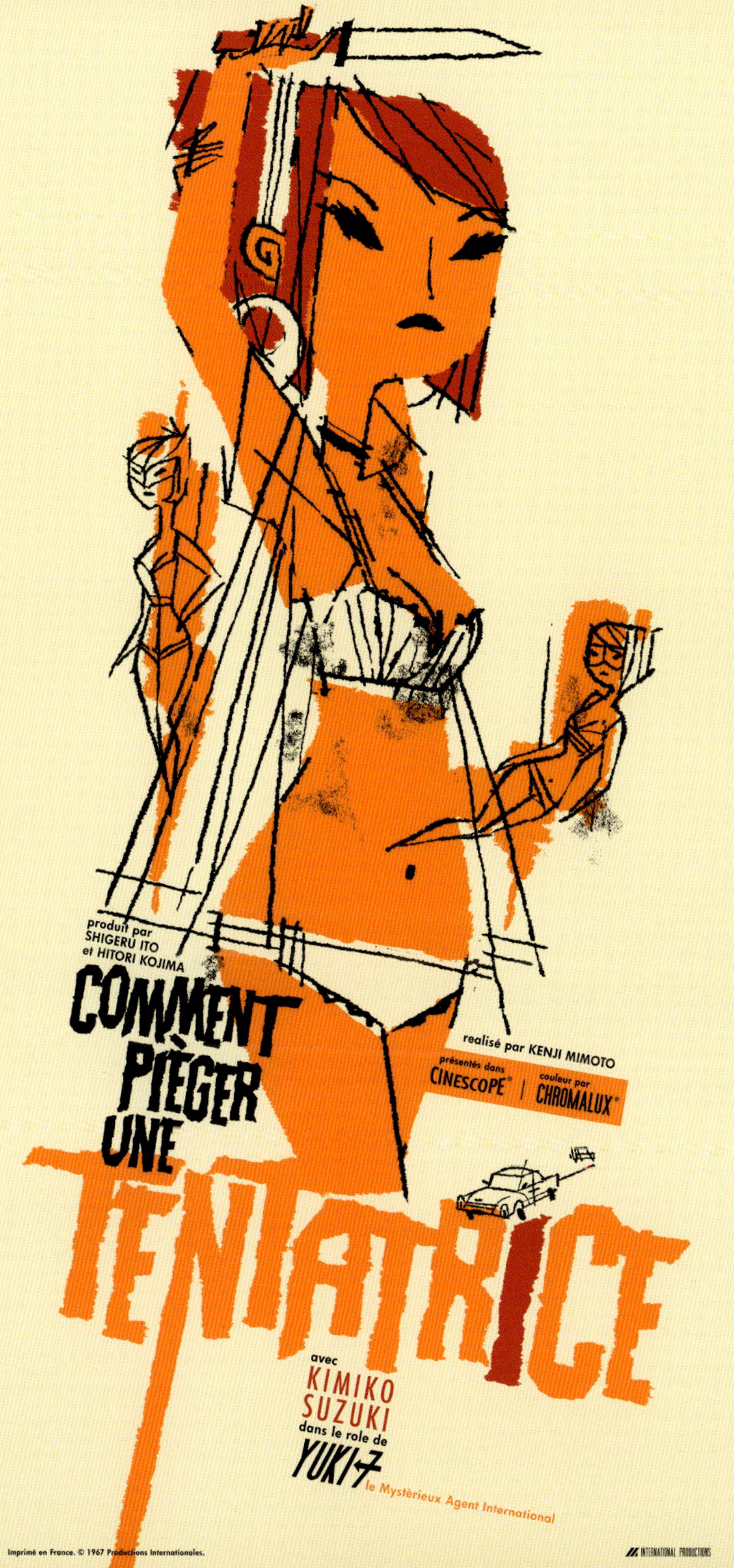

produit par
SHIGERU ITO
et HITORI KOJIMA
COMMENT
PIÈGER
UNE
TENTATRICE
realisé par KENJI MIMOTO
présentés dans
CINESCOPE®
couleur par
CHROMALUX®
avec
KIMIKO
SUZUKI
dans le role de
YUKI 7
le Mystèrieux Agent International
Imprimé en France. © 1967 Productions Internationales.
INTERNATIONAL PRODUCTIONS

1968
and Beyond

After the first four films were released, the world of Yuki 7 took on a life of its own. Fans across the globe had an unquenchable thirst for Yuki's irresistible charm, and the entertainment industry filled screens, magazines, and books with more of the beloved spy girl. Creative minds everywhere were inspired by the intelligent and sexy heroine, and Yuki 7 continued confidently toward a very bright future. The following pages feature selected memorabilia from this exciting era.

SANDY 6 PREPARES TO SEDUCE AND MURDER ANOTHER SCIENTIST
"A KISS FROM TOKYO" FILM STILL, 1964
Courtesy of Stephane Coedel, Cinematographer

YUKI 7

Murder 殺害 *in Milan* ミラノ

directed by
kenji-miroto
INTERNATIONAL PRODUCTIONS

presented in
CINESCOPE
THE ASTOUNDING
VIEWING EXPERIENCE

COLOR BY
CHROMALUX

Kimiko Suzuki as
YUKI 7
the Mysterious Agent

1968

Secret Agent Yuki 7 travels to Milan in pursuit of Toshiro Shindo, the famed Japanese fashion designer with a penchant for murder and mind control. He holds the fashion district hostage with an army of deadly runway models, and Yuki crawls the catwalk in disguise to unravel his devious plans.

◄ MURDER IN MILAN, Courtesy of Josh Parpan, Illustrator

DIAMOND IN THE ROUGH 1970

Money is pouring out of the glittering casinos on the coast of Monte Carlo, and the owners are desperate to discover how. It's the classic crime of card counting, but this time, the stakes are high and the culprits invisible. Yuki 7 infiltrates a cartel and encounters a familiar face. It's Diamond Eye, the Polynesian beauty with a talent for science and a penchant for lawlessness. When Diamond Eye doesn't blow Yuki's cover, Yuki sets out to answer a burning question - is her rival is behind the conspiracy or enslaved by the true mastermind?

◄ DIAMOND IN THE ROUGH, Courtesy of Don Shank, Illustrator
▲ DIAMOND IN THE ROUGH PAPERBACK COVER, Courtesy of Sinset Books

The Tokio Rose

1969

The legendary Tokio Rose, a powerful precious gem, has been stolen. Yuki unravels the tangled plot woven by infamous Russian mastermind Cake Hat and his conniving cohort Inga. Yuki chases down the jewel and defeats a skeleton army in a non-stop romp around romantic, sparkling Tokyo.

TOKIO ROSE, Courtesy of Brigette Barrager, Illustrator ◀
THREE FINGERS OF INTRIGUE, Courtesy of Scott Morse, Illustrator ▶

THREE FINGERS of INTRIGUE

1968

A daring double agent - codenamed Titus - is making his way through the Balkans, carrying with him a deadly secret. After a midnight boat ride across the stormy Adriatic sea and a climb into the beautiful limestone mountains of Montenegro, Yuki 7 finally discovers his hiding place. Titus has a weakness for lovely women and expensive liquor, and when femme fatale Yuki 7 turns on the charm and pours him three fingers of contraband whiskey, it doesn't take her long to discover where his alliances lie.

The Savage
Island of Dr.
Calamari
1975

Secret Agent Yuki 7 is dispatched to Greece after a fleet of nuclear submarines vanishes in the waters of the Aegean Sea. The mystery leads Yuki to the remote island base of Dr. Calamari, a French oceanographer who controls the predators of the deep with his strange and unnatural sciences. Using his legion of underwater monsters, the doctor is capturing the world's war machines and using them to create an atomic super weapon. He calls it "Manta Ray" and he plans to use it to flood entire continents. Yuki 7 must stop the Doctor before he initiates a terrifying age of aquatic dominance upon the world!

◄ THE ISLAND OF DR. CALAMARI, Courtesy of Justin Parpan, Illustrator

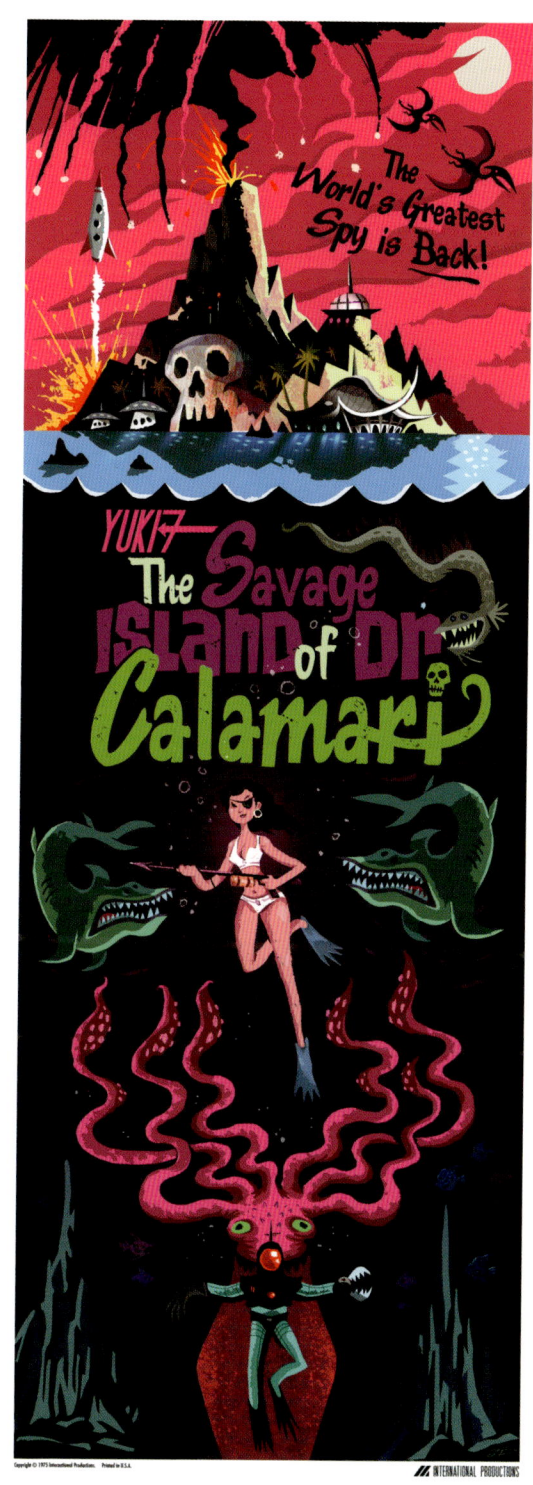

SHIGERU and HITORI ITO KOJIMA PRESENT **KENJI MIMOTO'S**

ONE WAY to DIE®

STARRING
KIMIKO SUZUKI
AS
SECRET AGENT
YUKI-7

1972

A conspiracy spans the globe, but top agent Yuki 7 finds out that it is deeply rooted dangerously close to home. Posing as a deadly assassin, Yuki infiltrates a notorious ninja crime syndicate. Can Yuki's cunning keep her alive?

◄ **ONE WAY TO DIE,** Courtesy of Horia Dociu, Illustrator

小島一人 提供

監督

kevin dart's

production journal

Yuki 7 was born in the Spring of 2008, when I returned from working in London. Venturing abroad for a bit helped me to see outside myself, and really got me thinking in detail about what inspires me as an artist. I started a list of things I found inspiring, but I felt were missing from my more recent work. For example, I decided that I wanted to be more deliberate about creating a story within my paintings. Once I discovered the story and the character, the ideas began flowing

in a way I had never experienced before. Yuki 7 unified all of the ideas and interests I had before into a single, focused project.

I started going to a local coffee shop, putting on some music, and sketching thumbnails. The ideas just seemed to flow endlessly, and after a few weeks I had a complete vision of the project in my mind. Once I had this pile of ideas, they began to evolve and fall into place, creating a

structure for the book. You can see the notes I made to divide my ideas into four movies and to define the style I wanted to use for the posters.

Once I determined what type of posters I would do, I did thumbnails. Here you can see a thumbnail evolve into a loose pencil sketch. Once the elements are arranged, I do a tone study to unite the piece and give me an idea where I can lay the colors I have in mind. The color study brings

CONTINUED ▶

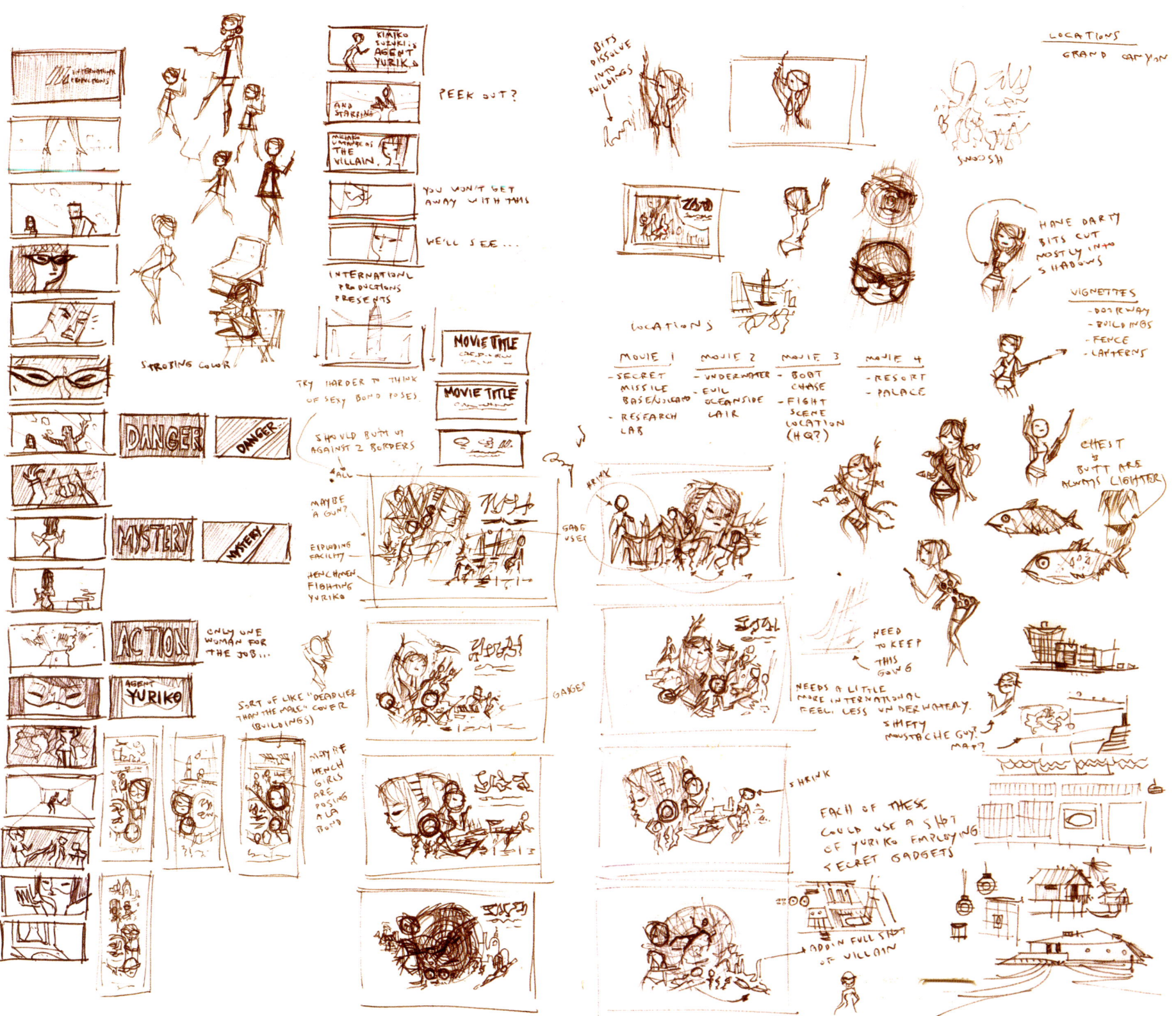

KIATKO SUZUKI's
AGENT YURIKO

PEEK OUT?

AND STARRING

MICHIKO UMURA as THE VILLAIN.

YOU WON'T GET AWAY WITH THIS

WE'LL SEE...

INTERNATIONAL PRODUCTIONS PRESENTS

STROBING COLOR

TRY HARDER TO THINK OF SEXY BOND POSES.

MOVIE TITLE

MOVIE TITLE

SHOULD BUTT UP AGAINST 2 BORDERS

MAYBE A GUN?

EXPLODING FACILITY

HENCHMEN FIGHTING YURIKO

ONLY ONE WOMAN FOR THE JOB...

SORT OF LIKE "DEADLIER THAN THE MALE" COVER (BUILDINGS)

MAYBE IF HENCH GIRLS ARE POSING A LA BOND

DANGER

MYSTERY

ACTION

AGENT YURIKO

BITS DISSOLVE INTO BUILDINGS

SWOOSH

LOCATIONS
GRAND CANYON

HAVE DARK BITS CUT MOSTLY INTO SHADOWS

VIGNETTES
- DOORWAY
- BUILDINGS
- FENCE
- LANTERNS

LOCATIONS

MOVIE 1	MOVIE 2	MOVIE 3	MOVIE 4
-SECRET MISSILE BASE/VOLCANO	-UNDERWATER EVIL OCEANSIDE LAIR	-BOAT CHASE	-RESORT
-RESEARCH LAB		-FIGHT SCENE LOCATION (HQ?)	-PALACE

DRINK

GADGET USE?

GADGET

NEED TO KEEP THIS GOING

NEEDS A LITTLE MORE INTERNATIONAL FEEL. LESS UNDERWATER. SHIFTY MOUSTACHE GUY? MAP?

CHEST & BUTT ARE ALWAYS LIGHTER

SHRINK

EACH OF THESE COULD USE A SHOT OF YURIKO EMPLOYING SECRET GADGETS

ADD IN FULL SHOT OF VILLAIN

the poster to life, and allows me to ensure that the colors I have chosen will all work together in the overall composition. From this point, I begin my final painting. Although I am building on my original plan, everything is still flexible and I adjust the elements on a much more detailed level.

Finally, I add small logos and details to imitate real movie posters. Chromalux, International Pro-

ductions, and the other logos are my own invention, along with the custom type I use for the movie titles.

From thumbnail to final painting, the time I spent on *Seductive Espionage: The World of Yuki 7* resulted in some of the most rewarding work that I have ever done.

HAVE LOTS OF LINE OVERLAYS?

AGENT LOTUS of IL ESPIONAGE ITALIANS

2 DRESSES
SCUBA
ROBE

DO A MODEL SHEET FOR YURIKO IN EACH COSTUME —

+ WEAPON DETAILS

3/4 FRONT PROFILE

VILLAINS: DO ONE STANDING POSE FOR H

SPECIAL AGENT LOTUS
VILLANO LADY
UNDERWATER LADY
MASKED LADY
MINOR VILLAINS!
ASSASSINS
HENCHMEN

ITALIAN POSTERS CAN
BE SCREENPRINT-STYLIZED
LIKE FRENCH REVOLUTION
POSTERS
3 COLORS
USE OVERLAP TO CREATE 4th
LINEWORK ISN'T FILLED IN
EXCEPT FOR YURIKO

EVERYONE
SHOULD BE
SUPER CUTE
i.e. ...

SKEWED & ACTION-Y

THUMBNAILS AND
NOTES FOR CHARACTER
DESIGN AND POSTER
PLANNING ◄

OPPOSITE: STEP BY STEP
PROCESS SNAPSHOTS FOR
"A KISS FROM TOKYO"
POSTER ►

❶ THUMBNAIL

❷ ROUGH PENCIL SKETCH

❸ TONE STUDY

❹ COLOR STUDY

❺ FINAL PAINTING

KEVIN DART

Yuki 7 began as a fleeting spark of inspiration in my head, but she was brought to life with the help and support of a huge group of my close friends. All of the world-class artists in this book gave me the amazing opportunity to see her through another person's eyes, Ada Cole dove deep into the murky waters of my brain and discovered what makes Yuki tick, Stephane Coedel took my half-hatched ideas and made them sparkle and shine, and the source of my inspiration, Elizabeth Ito, kept me going the whole time.

A small sampling of all the amazing people who have supported my endeavors and Fleet Street Scandal from the very beginning: my awesome parents and sister, Aunt Linda, my grandfather, Aunt Kathy and Uncle Curt, Mark & Rita Turnham, Dan Cole, Ed & Anne Ito, Jeff & Sherri Haynie, Scott & Deeann Mayhew, Matt Lucas, Hugo Morales, Chris Sweet, Bobby Pontillas & Cheryl Jacob, and to all of our dedicated Fleet Street fans – thank you!

Finally, thank you to the friendly people at the Starbucks on Orange Grove, Saigon Noodle, Capri, the taco truck on Fair Oaks, Orochan, and Chin-Ma-Ya for all the drawing fuel.

ADA COLE

This book is dedicated to my mother, who read to me the books that made me want to write.

Being a part of the Yuki 7 project was exciting from day one. I am so thankful to have had the chance to work with Kevin, exchanging ideas almost daily and working closely to develop the articles, ads, and stories that offer a glimpse into the world of Yuki 7. Thank you, Kevin, for inviting me into Yuki's world.

I owe thanks to many more people, including: My mother, Taeyun Erickson, for giving me everything I ever needed to be successful. Ayric Dierenfeld, for enthusiastic encouragement and belly laughs when I need them most. Keri Secord, for practical advice at any hour. Macy Mayhew, for an unforgettable afternoon. Thanks also to my beloved mother-in-law Carolyn Cole, Grandma Lulu, Jeff and Sherri Haynie, and Chris Turnham who have each encouraged me in a vital and special way.

Most of all, my thanks - and my heart - belong to my incredible husband, Dan Cole: When I think about how much I love you, my heart goes, *Yippee!*

探偵YUKITŌ

WRATH AND RUIN

Published by Everlast Books

www.jamesmaxwell.com

ISBN-13: 978-0-646-71641-1

Cover design by EGA

Printed in the United States of America

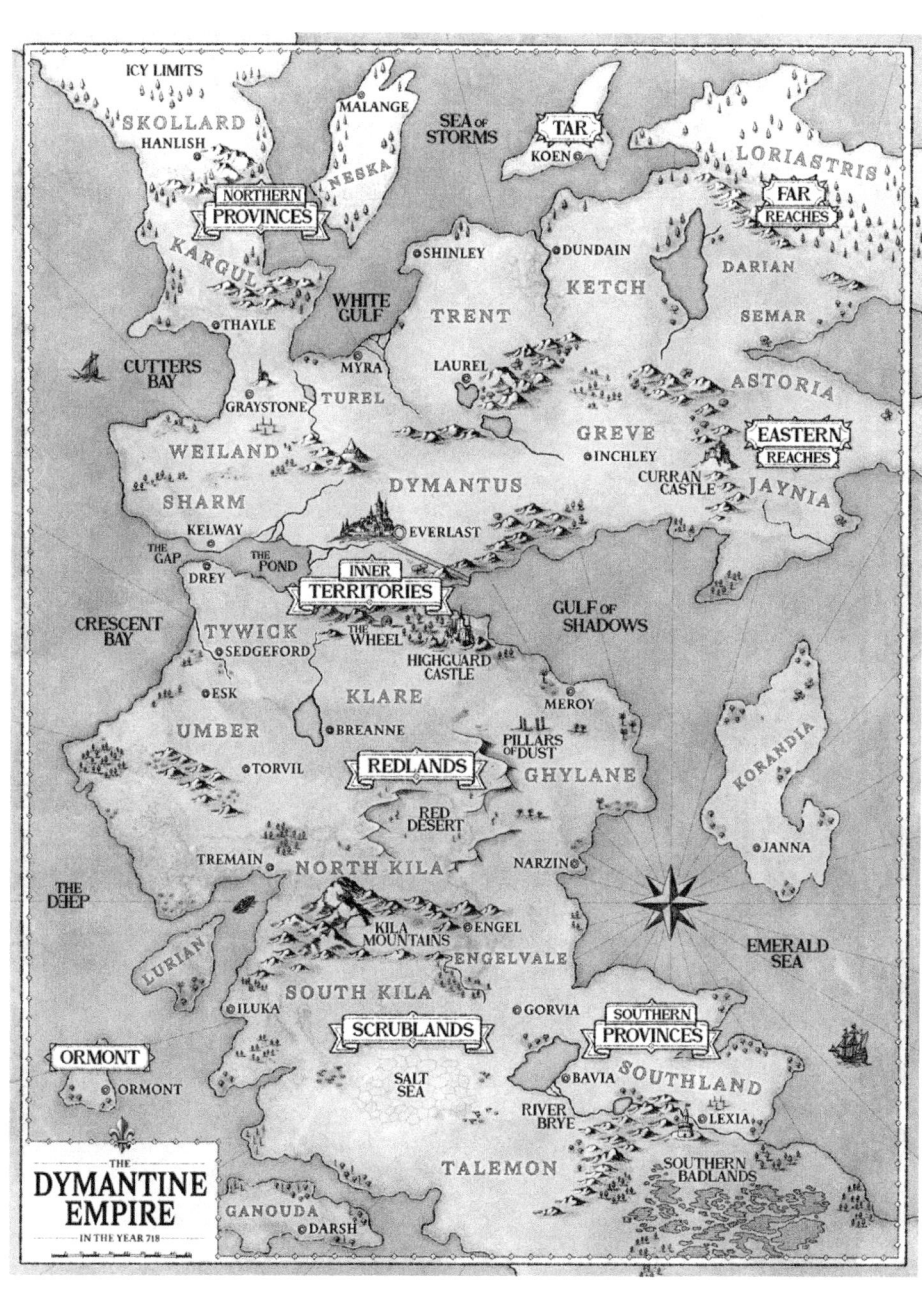

ICY LIMITS

SKOLLARD
HANLISH

MALANGE

SEA of STORMS

TAR
KOEN

LORIASTRIS

FAR
REACHES

NESKA

NORTHERN
PROVINCES

KARGUL

THAYLE

WHITE
GULF

SHINLEY

DUNDAIN

KETCH

DARIAN

SEMAR

CUTTERS
BAY

TRENT

MYRA

LAUREL

GRAYSTONE

TUREL

ASTORIA

WEILAND

GREVE
INCHLEY

EASTERN
REACHES

SHARM

DYMANTUS

CURRAN
CASTLE

JAYNIA

KELWAY

EVERLAST

THE
GAP

DREY

THE
POND

INNER
TERRITORIES

CRESCENT
BAY

TYWICK
SEDGEFORD

THE
WHEEL

GULF of
SHADOWS

ESK

HIGHGUARD
CASTLE

KLARE

MEROY

UMBER

BREANNE

PILLARS
of DUST

KORANDIA

TORVIL

REDLANDS

GHYLANE

RED
DESERT

TREMAIN

NORTH KILA

NARZIN

JANNA

THE
DEEP

LURIAN

KILA
MOUNTAINS

ENGEL

ENGELVALE

EMERALD
SEA

SOUTH KILA

ILUKA

SCRUBLANDS

GORVIA

SOUTHERN
PROVINCES

ORMONT

ORMONT

SALT
SEA

BAVIA

SOUTHLAND

RIVER
BRYE

LEXIA

THE
DYMANTINE
EMPIRE
IN THE YEAR 718

GANOUDA
DARSH

TALEMON

SOUTHERN
BADLANDS

For Alicia, with all my love and gratitude